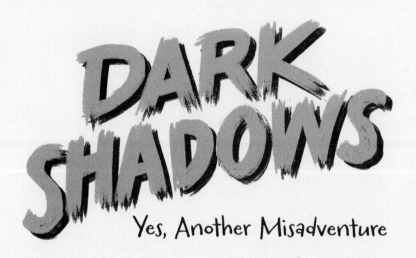

Yes, Another Misadventure

Also by Doreen Cronin

DARK SHADOWS

Yes, Another Misadventure

Doreen Cronin

Illustrated by Stephen Gilpin

Cover by Kevin Cornell

A Caitlyn Dlouhy Book

Atheneum Books for Young Readers

atheneum   New York   London   Toronto   Sydney   New Delhi

atheneum

ATHENEUM BOOKS FOR YOUNG READERS
An imprint of Simon & Schuster Children's Publishing Division
1230 Avenue of the Americas, New York, New York 10020
This book is a work of fiction. Any references to historical events, real people, or real places are used fictitiously. Other names, characters, places, and events are products of the author's imagination, and any resemblance to actual events or places or persons, living or dead, is entirely coincidental.
Text copyright © 2017 by Doreen Cronin
Case illustration (front) copyright © 2017 by Kevin Cornell
Case (back) and interior illustrations copyright © 2017 by Stephen Gilpin
All rights reserved, including the right of reproduction in whole or in part in any form.
ATHENEUM BOOKS FOR YOUNG READERS is a registered trademark of Simon & Schuster, Inc. Atheneum logo is a trademark of Simon & Schuster, Inc.
For information about special discounts for bulk purchases, please contact Simon & Schuster Special Sales at 1-866-506-1949 or business@simonandschuster.com.
The Simon & Schuster Speakers Bureau can bring authors to your live event. For more information or to book an event, contact the Simon & Schuster Speakers Bureau at 1-866-248-3049 or visit our website at www.simonspeakers.com.
Book design by Sonia Chaghatzbanian
The text for this book was set in Garth Graphic.
The illustrations for this book were rendered digitally.
Manufactured in the United States of America
0217 FFG
First Edition
10 9 8 7 6 5 4 3 2 1
CIP data for this book is available from the Library of Congress.
ISBN 978-1-4814-5049-2
ISBN 978-1-4814-5051-5 (eBook)

For Ken, Cathy, and Sean

—D. C.

For Noah

—S. G.

Yes, Another Misadventure

Introductions

In my search-and-rescue days, road trips meant danger, hard work, and with any luck, a rescue. My partner, Barbara, and I would hop in the car, hit the open road, and go wherever duty called. We didn't carry much more than a first-aid kit, some beef jerky, and a high-powered flashlight.

Now when we hit the road, we pack jelly beans, a bag of chicken feed, and a birdcage full of trouble:

Dirt: Short, yellow, fuzzy

Real Name: Peep

Specialty: Foreign languages, math, colors, computer codes

Sugar: Short, yellow, fuzzy

Real Name: Little Boo

Specialty: Breaking and entering,
interrupting

Poppy: Short, yellow, fuzzy

Real Name: Poppy

Specialty: Watching the shoe
(will explain later)

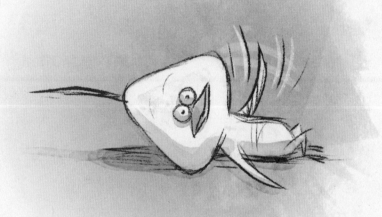

Sweetie: Short, yellow, fuzzy

Real Name: Sweet Coconut Louise

Specialty: None that I can see

Doreen Cronin

Well, it's been a long ride so far. I'm done sticking my head out the window. My neck hurts, and I have swallowed all the bugs I can handle in one day. Bugs are like doughnuts. One or two is just fine, but a dozen will give you a bad stomachache.

Chapter 1

The birdcage bounced around in the back of Barbara's old green station wagon. Dirt, Sugar, Poppy, and Sweetie bounced along inside of it in the storage area behind the backseat. By the time Barbara pulled off the main highway, it was after 6:00 p.m.

"Where are we going again?" asked Poppy.

"To a farm," answered J. J. from the backseat.

"What is the point of this trip again?" asked Sugar.

"To see things you've never seen before," said J. J.

"I've seen everything there is to see," said Sugar.

"You've barely been out of the backyard," said J. J.

"You have no idea where I've been, pal," said Sugar.

"Have you ever been to a farm, Mom?" asked Dirt.

"I grew up on the farm, silly!" answered Moosh.

"You grew up on a *farm?*" Sweetie gasped. "I had no idea!"

"We all have our secrets, kid," said Sugar. "Mom clearly has a dark past and doesn't want to talk about it. Let it go."

"I think you're all going to enjoy

it," Moosh continued. "There's wide-open space to run around, and there's even a pond! We can go fishing and swimming. . . ."

"I don't like to get wet," announced Sugar. "I'll just wait in the car."

"We can build a bonfire and sing songs," offered Moosh.

"I do have a beautiful singing voice," said Sugar. "I'll roll the window down a crack so you can hear me."

"We'll tell stories," added Moosh.

"Well, okay, I like a good story," said Sugar. "I'll stay in the car, but I'll roll down the window halfway so I can hear you."

"Can we toast marshmallows?" asked Dirt.

"That's a wonderful idea!" said Moosh.

"Okay," said Sugar. "I'll roll the window down almost all the way, but you'll need to bring me a really long stick so I can toast my marshmallow from the car."

"You can't stay in the car for a week," said J. J.

"You have no idea what I can do, pal," Sugar responded.

"The best part," continued Moosh, "is that you're going to meet your whole family—cousins, aunts, uncles. It's a family reunion!"

13

"There's more of us?" asked Dirt.

"There's more of them?" asked J. J.

"Of course!" replied Moosh.

"How many more?" asked J. J.

"Look for yourselves!" answered Moosh.

The car had turned off the road and was moving slowly down a long, muddy driveway toward a two-story yellow house. Gathered on the front porch and spilling over onto the steps and into the driveway were excited, gabbling chickens in every size, shape, and color.

"I've never seen so many chickens!" exclaimed Poppy.

14

"I'll be in the car with Sugar," growled J. J., covering his eyes with his paws.

Chapter 2

"We're here!" announced Barbara. She walked around to the back of the car, popped open the hatch, and gently placed the birdcage on the ground. "Welcome to the farm!" She grabbed her backpack, opened the birdcage door, and headed toward the house. "Make yourselves at home."

J. J. jumped out of the hatch and bolted toward the wide, grassy field. Moosh sprung out right behind him and then made a beeline for the front porch to reunite with her sisters. Dirt, Poppy, and Sweetie hopped out of the open birdcage and waited for Sugar to join them.

"Well?" prodded Dirt.

"I have a weird feeling," said Sugar. "I can't put my finger on it."

"Oh-kay," Dirt said slowly. "What kind of weird feeling?"

"It's called instinct, kid," answered Sugar.

"Oh-kay," Dirt said slowly again.

"Do you feel it now?" asked Sugar.

"Feel what?" asked Dirt.

"The weird feeling?" Sugar insisted.

"Yes," replied Dirt. "A mob of awkwardly silent chicken cousins is staring at us now. And you're right, that does feel really weird." Dirt turned to

the crowd and gave them a small wave. "Be right with you!"

J. J. trotted back to the cage. "Well?"

"Sugar feels weird," explained Dirt.

"Sugar *is* weird," sighed J. J. He shrugged and ran back toward the open fields.

"Are you afraid of new places too?" asked Sugar. "You can have my shoe: I always take it with me when I feel a little bit scared. It's right here in the car."

"Who said anything about being scared?" asked Sugar. "I just—"

"Come on, Sugar!" Moosh called, emerging from the family flock on the porch. "Come meet your cousins! They're all so excited!!"

"Coming, Mom!" Sugar reluctantly left the cage and trudged to the front porch with Poppy, Sweetie, and Dirt.

Before the first cousin could open his mouth, a Moosh look-alike appeared next to Moosh and blew into a whistle hanging around her neck. "Line up! Single file! No talking! Take your places!"

Dirt and Sugar exchanged glances. "Like we practiced!" said the Moosh look-alike. The chaotic mob of porch chickens was now an orderly single-file line that wrapped all the way around the house. They marched past the chicken squad and nodded hello, giving their names one at a time.

"Bailey."

"Bassie."

"Beatrice."

"Belle."

"Bernadette."

"Bert."

Sugar, Dirt, Poppy, and Sweetie nodded politely at each chicken as they politely introduced themselves, with no end in sight. After the first few minutes, Moosh and the Moosh-look-alike whistling chicken climbed back to the porch to catch up with their sisters.

"How are we ever going to remember all of their names?" cried Poppy. "I don't want to be rude!"

"They're in alphabetical order," answered Dirt. "And I'm writing them all down."

"They all have *B* names, kid," said Sugar. "You can't alphabetize words that start with the same letter." The chicken squad continued to nod and smile as their cousins announced their names.

"If the first letter is the same, you use the second letter to alphabetize," explained Dirt. "And then the third, so on and so . . ."

"Betsy."

"Bibi."

"Bichon."

"Biden."

"Biff."

"This *B* business is going to take all

day!" moaned Sugar. "I'm going back to the car to get a snack."

"You can't leave in the middle of introductions," Poppy protested. "That's so rude!"

"You only have to have manners when Mom is watching. Don't you know anything?" Sugar took a quick

look around. "What I need is a decoy. Bring me a loofah sponge, a hot glue gun, and six yards of yellow chiffon. . . ."

"We don't have any of those things," replied Dirt, still nodding and smiling as their cousins filed past them.

"Fine," said Sugar, "we'll do it the easy way." Sugar used her feet to

gather the loose chicken feathers on the ground into a pile in front of her, until it was higher than she was tall.

"That is never going to work," said Dirt.

Sugar took off her glasses and placed them on the pile.

"Perfect!" she declared. Then she ducked behind it and headed back to the car.

"Bladimir."

"Blaire."

"Blake."

"Bring back some jelly beans!" Dirt called after her.

"Blanca."

"Blanche."

"Blane."

"*B* right back," Sugar answered, cracking herself up as she hurried away.

Chapter 3

Sugar hopped up into the open car and rummaged around the back searching for the jelly beans. "Would be a lot easier with my glasses," she mumbled as she tossed things out of her way and out of the car. "AHA!" She pulled the bag of jelly beans out from under the fishing gear and had just popped a red jelly bean into her mouth and plopped herself down next to Poppy's shoe when she sensed someone behind her. She turned around, but no one was there.

"*Ha-hoo, ha-hoo, ha-hoo.*" Sugar stopped chewing when she heard

the sound of someone breathing. She swallowed her half-chewed jelly bean in one gulp. As she peered around the edge of the car, a long, dark shadow appeared at her feet. Her eyes went wide. Her heart raced. "Who's there?" she demanded, spinning around for a

second time. The shadow was gone.

"Step away from the vehicle," said a deep voice from behind her *again*. "Slowly, and with your hands up." Sugar turned around, slowly, with her wings up, to find a large speckled chicken with a wide face, enormous eyes, and a long gray string hanging out of its mouth, standing in the spot where, not one second ago, there had been nobody.

"Take it easy, pal," Sugar replied. "Just grabbing my jelly beans."

"Those jelly beans do not belong to you," answered the large chicken. "They belong to the visiting cousins.

Now do as I say and step away from the vehicle."

"Ah, just a misunderstanding." Sugar chuckled nervously, taking two giant steps backward. "I *am* one of the visiting cousins."

"No, you're not," boomed the large chicken. "I met them already. One's got a pointy head; one's got a notebook

and a pencil; one has a big, round face; and the last one barely looks like a pile of feathers, she's so tiny. Cute little thing with glasses."

"That's me," insisted Sugar. "*I'm* the cute one! Really, I just ducked away for a—"

"There's nothing cute about you," declared the large chicken. "And

besides, the cute one wore glasses."
He picked Sugar up with an incredibly
sharp pinch of his toes and held her
off the ground. "I just checked, and all
four cousins are still up by the house.
They'll be making polite introductions
for a good long while. There's another
eighty-five more chickens to go until
they get to the end of the line."

"That's exactly why you don't recog-
nize me," said Sugar, quickly hatching
a new plan.

"I know family when I see it." The
large speckled chicken with the wide
face, enormous eyes, and a long gray
string hanging out of his mouth pulled

Sugar in closer to get a better look. "And I do *not* know you."

"Well, like you said, it's an awfully big family," Sugar declared. "Although, I'll admit, it kind of hurts my feelings that you don't remember me. We played together once . . . down by the . . . pond."

"We did? What's your name?" asked the large chicken, looking confused.

Sugar thought of all the cousins she had met earlier. "My name is . . . Bugar." She regretted saying it immediately.

"Booger?" But the large speckled chicken with the wide face, enormous eyes, and the long gray string hanging

out of his mouth didn't laugh. "Who's
your mom, Booger?"

"She's the big one . . . with white
feathers . . . and small black eyes.
Looks just like her sisters. She might
be upset if I told her you roughed me
up. Might tell the other moms, too.

I'd hate for that to happen. Wouldn't you?"

The large speckled chicken with the wide face, enormous eyes, and the long gray string hanging out of his mouth placed Sugar gently back down on the ground.

Sugar brushed herself off. "You didn't tell me *your* name."

"Frizzle," answered the chicken.

"Frizzle?" repeated Sugar suspiciously. "Why don't you have a *B* name like everybody else?"

"Did I say Frizzle? I meant Befrizzle," said the large speckled chicken with the wide face, enormous eyes, and

a long gray string hanging out of his mouth. "Frizzle is my . . . nickname."

"Befrizzle, huh?" repeated Sugar. "I don't think I trust you, Befrizzle." Sugar narrowed her eyes before turning on her heel to walk away.

"I keep an eye on things around here, Booger. I watch things. I see things. I know things," added Befrizzle. "And I *know* you don't belong anywhere near that car."

"Nobody tells Bugar where she belongs, pal. Bugar can be anywhere. Under your seat, on your pillow, even right under your nose." She regretted saying it immediately. "What I meant to say . . . Befrizzle?" she called. But Befrizzle was gone.

And so were the jelly beans.

Chapter 4

Sugar crawled into the pile of decoy feathers. Her glasses fell into place and the feathers fell to the ground around her. She nodded as the last of the chickens made their introductions.

"Buddy."

"Bunk."

"Buster."

"It's about time!" Dirt cried. "Did you bring the jelly beans?

"The jelly beans are gone," Sugar answered.

"You ate two bags of jelly beans?" Dirt cried.

"There were two?" asked Sugar. "I only saw one!"

"We always hide one from you," said Sweetie.

"I can't believe you ate all the jelly beans!" complained Poppy.

"I can't believe you have a secret bag!" Sugar complained right back. "Anyway, I didn't eat them! Cousin Befrizzle took them!"

"Butter."

"Butterball."

"Cousin who?" asked Dirt.

"Buzz."

"Buzzy."

"Befrizzle," answered Sugar. "Some kind of chicken security guard or something. Followed me back to the car, accused me of stealing, and then disappeared with the jelly beans! Unbelievable!"

"Um, Sugar," said Dirt, checking her list of cousins. "There is no Cousin Befrizzle."

"What do you mean?" said Sugar.

"If we had a cousin named Befrizzle," said Dirt, "he would have been in line right here between Beatrice and Belle. See for yourself."

"Maybe he just got bored and skipped the introductions," said Sugar.

"That would be very rude," said Poppy.

"I did it," replied Sugar.

"Like I said," answered Poppy, shooting his sister a look.

"I am telling you guys," said Sugar. "Befrizzle is our cousin, and he is a large speckled chicken with a wide face, enormous eyes, and a long gray string hanging out of his mouth."

"You do realize that description is pretty strange and that name sounds completely made up, right?" asked Dirt.

"Believe it or not, you may be on to something, Dirt!" said Sugar. "Granted, I didn't have my glasses on, but there was definitely something off about Befrizzle. Something my street smarts and chicken instincts picked up on. I think he may have pretended to be something he's not just to get to those jelly beans!"

"Seems like a lot of work just to get some jelly beans," remarked Sweetie.

"Plus, that would be really rude."

"A big chicken with a dark heart will stop at nothing to get jelly beans!" declared Sugar.

Dirt let out a heavy sigh. "Okay, Sugar. We'll go back up to the car and see if anything else is out of place." She turned to Poppy and Sweetie. "Come on, guys, let's look around."

"For what?" asked Poppy.

"I'm not sure," whispered Dirt.

"Evidence!" shouted Sugar.

"What kind of evidence?" asked Dirt.

"Hair, fibers, paint chips, glass fragments!" shouted Sugar. "The usual!"

Dirt paused. "Okay, Sugar, let's go see if *Bedrazzle* left any *paint chips* or *fibers* behind. Right, guys?" She winked at Poppy and Sweetie.

"Be*frizzle*!" said Sugar, exasperated.

"The more you say it, the more made up it sounds," Dirt said, and they headed for the car.

Chapter 5

As Dirt, Sugar, Poppy, and Sweetie walked toward the car, their cousins lined up, single file, and followed behind. "What are we going to do about them?" asked Sweetie under her breath.

Dirt stopped for a moment, considered the hundred or so chicken cousins standing behind them, and then felt her stomach gurgle. "I think we will be saved by the bell."

"Cousin Belle?" asked Poppy.

"Wait for it," replied Dirt.

Sure enough, the dinner bell rang, and the line of chickens reversed direction and sped to the barnyard. Sugar, Poppy, Dirt, and Sweetie continued up the driveway.

"That's a very long dinner line," observed Dirt. "It will be at least an hour before anybody realizes we're not at the end of it."

"I found something!" yelled Sweetie. "Over here! I found something! It's a

giant shoe print!" The squad gathered at the back of the car.

"Wait a minute!" cried Poppy, running in circles inside the car. "Where's my shoe? It was right here! MY SHOE IS GONE!" Poppy leaped out and tackled Sugar. "WHAT DID YOU DO WITH MY SHOE?"

"It must have fallen out of the car when I was looking for jelly beans," Sugar answered. "Take it easy!"

"You said Cousin Besnickle took the jelly beans!" said Poppy, pointing a finger in Sugar's face.

"Befrizzle!! B-E-F-R— Never mind! This is a crime scene! The first thing we need to do is secure the area! Bring me a roll of police tape, some orange cones, and a high-definition camera!"

"We don't have any of those things," answered Dirt.

"Fine, we'll do it the easy way," said Sugar. "Try not to step on anything."

"I can't sleep without my shoe!"

cried Poppy, his lower beak quivering. "It's almost dark and I'm in a new place and I need my shoe!"

"I promise I will get your shoe back," said Sugar.

"And the jelly beans," added Sweetie. "Don't forget the jelly beans."

"Believe it or not, I think you're on to something, Sweetie!" declared Sugar. "Since Befrizzle likes taking jelly beans from small, defenseless chickens so much, maybe he'll come looking for more. . . ."

Poppy, Sweetie, and Dirt gathered in

a circle around Sugar. "All we need is a decoy to lure Befrizzle back to the scene," said Sugar. "Bring me a loofah sponge, a hot glue gun, and six yards of yellow chiffon."

"We *still* don't have any of those things," sighed Dirt. "Can't we just

make a decoy out of loose feathers like you did before?"

"Are you sure you didn't pack fabric and loofah sponges for the farm trip?" asked Sugar.

"Positive," sighed Dirt.

"Fine, we'll do it the easy way," said Sugar. "Grab up all the loose chicken feathers down by the house." She turned to Dirt. "And from now on, I do all the packing. Is that understood?"

Dirt let out another heavy sigh.

Chapter 6

Shortly after sunset, Sugar, Dirt, Poppy, and Sweetie peeked out the rear window of the station wagon. All eyes were on the decoy sitting in the birdcage just a few feet away, the secret second bag of jelly beans lying beside it.

"How is this going to work again?" asked Poppy.

Dirt rolled out her diagram. "We have the fishing line hooked up to the door of the birdcage. When Bepizzle tries to—"

"Be*frizzle!*" snapped Sugar.

"Fine," continued Dirt. "When *Befrizzle*

tries to grab the jelly beans out of the cage, we pull back on the fishing pole and *BLAM*—we've got him in the cage. We won't let him out until he tells us where the shoe is."

"This is taking too long," said Sugar. "I'm going outside."

"What are you going to do? You'll blow our cover!" asked Dirt.

"I'm going to secure the perimeter," answered Sugar.

"Secure the *what?*" asked Poppy.

"The *perimeter*," answered Sugar.

"What's a *perimeter*?" asked Sweetie.

"Listen, kid." Sugar chuckled. "*Perimeter* is a very complicated term that would take about six hours to properly explain. We simply don't have the time right—"

"A perimeter is the distance around something," interrupted Dirt. "If you drew a rectangle around the car, that would be the perimeter."

"I'd estimate the perimeter to be around one mile," said Sugar. "I'll be back in an hour."

"I don't think that's right," said Dirt.

"It's just an estimate, kid," explained Sugar. "It doesn't need to be *exact*!"

"It should actually be kind of close,"

explained Dirt. "We just need to add." She took out some crayons and drew a rectangle. "The car is about ten feet long and five feet wide. So . . ."

"There is a time and a place for everything!" cautioned Sugar. "And the dark of night is no time for math!"

"To find the perimeter, we just add up all the sides. So 10 + 5 + 10 + 5," continued Dirt. Poppy and Sweetie watched as Dirt set up her equation.

"This is scary!" said Poppy. "What if we get it wrong?"

"It's okay to get things wrong," said Dirt. "I get things wrong all the time."

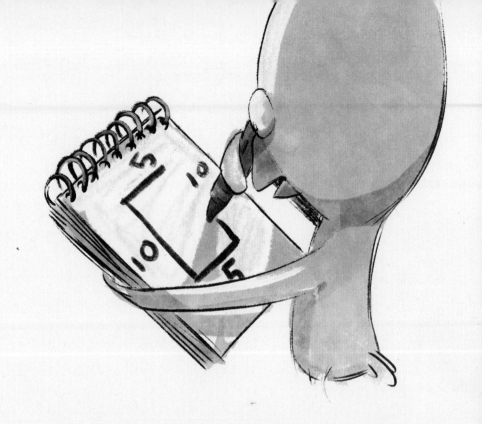

"You got that right," mumbled Sugar. "Let's start with your packing—"

"Okay, so 10 + 10 = 20," continued Dirt, ignoring Sugar's remark. "And 5 + 5 = 10."

"Don't come crying to me when your night math doesn't turn out the way you expect it to!" warned Sugar.

"And 20 + 10 = 30," finished Dirt. "It's approximately thirty feet around the car. So I'm going to estimate that it will take you just about a minute to secure the perimeter."

"Nice work, kid," said Sugar. "I'm proud of you. It takes nerves of steel to do math in the dark. I didn't think it could be done."

"Thanks, Sug—"

"Shhhh," said Sugar, her wing to her beak. She pressed her face against the window. "Something's out there. . . ."

Dirt took her position at the fishing pole and gripped it as tightly as she could.

Sugar motioned for Poppy and Sweetie to take cover under the front seat.

"Stay down!" she whispered. "It's coming closer."

Sugar grabbed a small shovel from Barbara's search-and-rescue kit and walked toward the front passenger window on shaky legs.

"Ha-hoo, ha-hoo, ha-hoo." Through the open crack, she could hear someone breathing. A shiver went down her spine. Sugar raised the shovel over her head.

"SHELP!!!"

Sugar and the shovel fell backward from the weight of the shovel, knocking everybody over. The squad helped one another to their feet, and Sugar scrambled to the top of the headrest. "The decoy is gone!" she exclaimed, gaping out the window.

"Did we catch Befrickle?" asked

Dirt. She ran to the window to get a closer look.

"Negative," said Sugar, alarmed. "And the cage is gone too."

"That's impossible!" cried Dirt.

The chickens ran up the fishing pole and slid down the fishing line outside the window.

"No paint chips and no fibers," noted Sugar.

"No footprints, either," noted Dirt with an eye roll.

"Nothing but some loose feathers," observed Sweetie. "They must have fallen off the decoy."

"Our decoy was covered in *yellow*

feathers," said Sugar. "But this one's white and speckled. AHA! Bring me a pair of tweezers, an evidence bag, and a high-powered microscope. STAT!"

"We don't have any of those things," Dirt declared.

"Fine, we'll do it the easy way," said

Sugar. "Put it in your pocket and try not to bend it."

"Now what?" asked Poppy.

"This is tough to say, kid, and even tougher to hear. It's late, it's dark, and we're in a strange place with a jelly bean–taking, shoe-stealing, abnormally large chicken on the loose, and there is nobody here to help us. We are absolutely, completely, and totally on our own."

"Couldn't we just ask Mom?" said Dirt.

"I'm sure J. J. would help," added Sweetie.

"Or the cousins? They seemed nice.

I'm sure they might help," suggested Poppy.

"We can help you, Booger," said a pair of voices from under the car. "We know where your shoe is."

The chicken squad peered under the car. Four red eyes, parked low to the ground, peered back out at them.

"Who's Booger?" asked Dirt, Poppy, and Sweetie in unison.

"She's Booger," said the voices, their eyes shifting together in Sugar's direction.

"Who are *you*?" asked Dirt, turning back to the eyes.

"We're just piglets under the car," they said together.

"How do you know my name?" asked Sugar.

"Huh?" said Dirt, Poppy, and Sweetie, turning to stare at their sister.

"I needed a new name in a hurry," Sugar explained. "And I picked Bugar!" She regretted saying it immediately.

Chapter 7

"Instinct tells me we probably shouldn't trust piglets under the car," said Dirt.

"The same instincts that helped you pack?" asked Sugar. "Listen, kid, we're on a *farm*. Piglets under cars are perfectly normal." She turned her attention back to the pigs. "How do you know where to find the shoe?"

"We keep an eye on things around here, Booger. We watch things. We see things. We know things," answered the piglets. "And we *know* where your shoe is."

"I thought Bespackled was the security guard around here," asked Poppy, confused.

"Never mind that!" cried Sugar.

"So," said Dirt, "where's the shoe?"

"Not so fast," said the piglets. "You give us something *we* want, and then we give you something *you* want."

"What is it you want, exactly?" asked Sugar.

"A loofah sponge, a hot glue gun, and six yards of yellow chiffon," said the piglets under the car.

Sugar narrowed her eyes and spun to face Dirt. "NEVER . . . PACKING . . . AGAIN! Do you hear me?"

"We don't have any of those

things," said Dirt, embarrassed.

"Fine," answered the piglets together. "We want jelly beans."

"We don't have any more jelly beans," replied Sugar. "Befrizzle took the first bag *and* the secret second bag, too."

"Tough bit of luck there, Booger," said the piglets under the car. "I guess we can't help you with that shoe, after all."

"There's actually a third bag, Booger. I mean, Sugar," said Dirt.

"What?" yelped Sugar.

"There's a *super*-secret third bag of jelly beans. In case of an emergency."

"You've been withholding jelly beans this whole time?" Sugar cried. "And you call yourselves *family*?"

"I'm sorry, but you're not a good sharer, Sugar Booger!" squeaked Sweetie. "There, I finally said it!"

"Had to be said," agreed the piglets.

Dirt hopped up into the car and then reappeared with the super-secret third bag of jelly beans.

"Toss it," said the piglets.

Dirt tossed the jelly beans under the car into the dark.

"Your shoe is in the barn. High up in the rafters. With family." Then the piglets closed their eyes and the area under the car went completely black and silent.

Chapter 8

The chicken squad peeked through the crack between the big red double doors. "Now remember, the plan is that we're going to search the barn, interrogate the cousins, find Befrizzle, and then he'll take us to the shoe," Sugar reminded them.

"Mom is not going to just let us

interrogate our cousins," said Dirt.

"That *is* a really rude thing to do," added Sweetie.

"Not if Mom doesn't see it!" whispered Sugar as they tiptoed in the shadows. "Now keep it down or you'll wake the—"

"There you are!" The squad looked back and saw half a dozen wide-awake chickens gathered around the old tractor parked inside the barn. They all looked exactly like Moosh.

"Which one is Mom?" whispered Dirt.

"No idea," replied Sugar. "It may be a trap. Let me handle this. . . ."

"You are so adorable!" said one of the chickens.

Sugar turned to her siblings. "That's not Mom."

"What sweet angels!" said another chicken.

"Absolutely not Mom," mumbled Sugar.

One of the chickens stepped forward with her wings on her hips. She nar-

rowed her eyes and took in a long, deep breath. Her chicken nostrils flared.

"That one's Mom," said Sugar.

"Your cousins have been looking all over for you," said Moosh. "They were finally so tuckered out they all went to bed!"

"We were playing hide-and-seek, Mom," fibbed Sugar. "Looks like we won!"

"Off to bed with you then!" said Moosh impatiently. "More time for fun and games in the morning." She walked them over to a soft spot of hay just a few feet from where she was visiting with her sisters.

"Aren't you going to sleep now too, Mom?" asked Sugar.

"Too much catching up to do!" answered Moosh, her voice suddenly happy again. "We'll probably talk until the sun comes up!"

Sugar and Dirt exchanged looks as they watched Moosh settle back down by the tractor, just a few feet away.

"They're going to be up all night!" moaned Poppy. "We'll never find Befrizzle, and I'm never going to get my shoe back!"

Sugar thought for a moment. "Dirt, come with me. Bring your notebook."

Sugar and Dirt stepped over to the

tractor. "Mom, can you help us with something?"

"What is it?" asked Moosh, eyeing them suspiciously.

"Well, the, um, the barn is feeling very BIG to Poppy so, um Dirt and I thought that if we could show him *exactly* how big it was, it would help

him fall asleep . . . ," explained Sugar as she motioned for Dirt to open her notebook. "You know how he doesn't really like new places. Right, Dirt?"

"Riiight," said Dirt. "So, um, can you help us figure out the perimeter of the barn?"

"So worried about their little brother," said one of the Moosh look-alikes. "I'd love to help!"

"Not Mom," Sugar mumbled to herself.

Dirt drew on her pad, sketching out the barn and estimating the length and width in feet. Then she labeled the sides of the barn and mapped out her equation. "So we just add 50 + 50 and 70 + 70 . . ."

"Shhh . . . ," said Sugar. Dirt looked up. All the grown-ups were sound asleep with their heads tucked beneath their wings.

"Wow," whispered Dirt.

"Night math," replied Sugar, walking over their bodies to get to her sister. "More than they could handle. They'll be out cold till morning."

"You scare me sometimes, Sugar," said Dirt.

"I scare myself sometimes too, kid."

Chapter 9

Sugar climbed the rungs up to the sleep-ing area, and the squad followed as quietly as they could. Their cousins were all sound asleep, lined up in neat rows.

"What brings you to the barn, Booger?" The giant chicken stepped out of the darkest corner on the highest row.

"Well, what have we here?" said

Sugar. "A large speckled chicken with a wide face, enormous eyes, and a long gray string hanging out of his mouth!"

"I'm pretty sure that's a mouse tail," said Dirt, moving in closer.

"Ew!" said Sweetie.

"I can see you clearly now, Befrizzle," said Sugar, stepping closer. "Very, very clearly. And you are no chicken."

"I never said—" Befrizzle began.

"Listen, kid," said Sugar. "You know exactly what you are, and I know exactly what you are. You're an . . . *emu*!"

"An emu?" said Dirt.

"A what-mu?" said Befrizzle, blinking rapidly.

"Why wouldn't he admit to being an emu?" asked Dirt.

"You're right, Dirt. My bad," said Sugar. "He's a SHEMU!"

"A shemu?" said Dirt. "What's a shemu?"

"It's the female form of emu," explained Sugar. "Like cow and bull, rooster and hen. Gander and goose.

You know . . . emu and shemu."

"I don't think that's right," said Dirt.

"I'll tell you what's not right," said Sugar. "Befrizzle is not right! He doesn't look like one of us; he doesn't even breathe like one of us!"

Dirt, Sweetie, and Poppy gasped.

"What's not right," Sugar continued, "is Befrizzle pretending to be part of our family so he could steal our jelly beans!"

Tears rolled down Befrizzle's exceptionally wide face.

"Why am I suddenly getting that weird feeling again?" asked Sugar.

"I'm pretty sure you get that feeling

whenever you're being, well, rude," suggested Sweetie.

"She's right," said Dirt. "Plus . . . a mob of awkwardly silent chickens has surrounded us, and that does feel really weird."

"Befrizzle is absolutely part of this family," said Bailey, Bassie, Bert, and Bodie. The chicken cousins all took

a step toward Sugar, pressing closer. Befrizzle wiped his tears with an enormous speckled wing.

"Oh no, poor Befrizzle," said Poppy. "Sugar didn't mean to be rude. She . . . just . . . well, *is*, sometimes!"

"Only when Mom's not around!" protested Sugar. "That doesn't really count!"

Befrizzle closed his eyes and took a deep, calming breath. "I think I know what you are looking for." He opened his expansive wings and took off into the rafters of the barn without making a sound. The chicken squad watched in awe. He landed silently a moment later with the cage and the feather decoy. "This little one looked so scared in the cage in the dark that I couldn't bear to leave her there alone. She hasn't said a word, but she's very sweet, and she's been keeping me company all night."

Sugar looked down at her feet.

"You can't sleep at night?" asked Dirt.

Befrizzle shook his head.

"Are you nocturnal?" Dirt asked gently.

Befrizzle nodded.

"Does that mean 'lonely'?" asked Poppy.

"No," said Dirt. "Animals that are awake mostly at night and sleep during the day are nocturnal. Like owls and mice." Dirt turned back to Befrizzle. "You're an owl, aren't you?"

Befrizzle nodded slowly.

"I bet it's kind of lonely being the only one up at night," said Poppy.

"It is," explained Befrizzle. "That's why I was so happy to have company.

Even if she was too afraid to come out of the cage."

"Um, w-well ... the thing is, Befrizzle," stammered Sugar, "that's just a pile of feathers we made as a decoy. . . ."

"You tricked Befrizzle?" cried the cousins.

"Wait, your *real* name *is* Befrizzle?" asked Sugar.

"Of course it is, Booger," said Befrizzle. "Why would I give you a fake name?"

Sugar shrugged, embarrassed.

"I'm sorry, Befrizzle," said Poppy. "And thank you for being so kind to our . . . decoy chicken."

Befrizzle opened the cage door. "Well, she didn't look like the rest of the chickens and she didn't act like the rest of the chickens and she was awful quiet, but I knew she was part of the family and I wanted her to feel safe and welcome." Befrizzle lowered his voice. "Even if she's not a real chicken, it was still nice to have someone stay up all night with me."

"We could take turns staying up all night with you," said Bailey, Bassie, Bert, and Bodie.

"You would?" asked Befrizzle. "But why?"

"Because you're family," said the

chickens. They gathered for a group hug.

"Befrizzle," Dirt said suddenly, "why aren't you on my alphabetical list of cousins?"

"I fell asleep," Befrizzle said shyly. "It happens a lot during the day."

Dirt wrote Befrizzle's name in her notebook list.

"I have your shoe," said a voice in the dark.

"Do not trust piglets in the dark!" cried Sugar. The chicken cousins went awkwardly silent again.

"Is that you, J. J.?" Dirt called out.

J. J. sat just at the bottom of the

ladder. "I was securing the perimeter when I heard some loud chewing and giggling coming from under the car. I hauled a couple of sugar-happy piglets out of the mud and found two empty jelly bean bags and Poppy's shoe under

there with them. Thought you might need it to sleep."

"I can't believe you trusted piglets under a car." Befrizzle chuckled. "Don't you have any farm smarts, Booger?"

"Booger?" said J. J.

"I picked it when nobody was around, and it just stuck!" answered Sugar. She regretted saying it immediately.

Epilogue

The entire chicken clan and two small pigs waved at us as we pulled out of the long dirt driveway a week later. Just like Moosh had promised, there had been fishing, swimming, a bonfire with marshmallows, and even a hayride sing-along for the whole family from chickens and owls to piglets, and even a few frogs from the pond. Poppy wants to know how soon we can visit again, and Sugar didn't want to get back in the car when it was time to go. The chicken cousins sleep in shifts now, and Befrizzle has plenty of company.

The fresh, clean farm air did wonders

for me, too. I slept like a baby. The wide-open space had reminded me of my younger days, and during the ride home, I entertained the chicken squad with story after story after— Hang on, Sugar has a question about the perimeter of the backyard at ho— *Zzzzzzzzzzzzz.*